Qui

Points 0.5

LITTLE WITCH GOES TO CAMP

By Deborah Hautzig

Illustrated by Sylvie Wickstrom

A Random House PICTUREBACK® Book

Random House New York

Library of Congress Cataloging-in-Publication Data:
Hautzig, Deborah.
Little Witch goes to camp / by Deborah Hautzig ; illustrated by Sylvie Wickstrom. p. cm. — (Pictureback)
SUMMARY: Little Witch goes to camp and is upset when she does not seem to fit in.
ISBN 0-679-87338-4 [1. Witches—Fiction. 2. Camps—Fiction. 3. Interpersonal relations—Fiction.] I. Wickstrom, Sylvie, ill. II. Title.
III. Random House pictureback. PZ7.H2888 Lie 2002 [E]—dc21 2001048755

www.randomhouse.com/kids

Printed in the United States of America First Edition May 2002 10 9 8 7 6 5 4 3 2 1

Little Witch could hardly wait! She was going to day camp for the very first time. Her pets helped her get ready. Her bat, Scrubby, brushed Little Witch's hair with both wings. Her cat, Bow-Wow, licked her black shoes till they gleamed.

Little Witch's friend Marcus was going, too. "I am lucky," Little Witch told Mother Witch. "I already have one friend at camp. And I will make *new* friends, too! Right?"

"Of course," grumbled Mother Witch. "Everybody always likes you. You're too NICE."

Mother Witch gave Little Witch a big bag of candy for lunch.

"Don't make too many friends," she warned.

"Have a rotten time!" said Aunt Grouchy.

"Be mean to EVERYBODY!" snarled Aunt Na

Cousin Dippy had a gift for Litt Witch.

"Here's a new bathing suit for y to fly in!" she said happily.

"Oh, thank you!" said Little Wit

"Cousin Dippy doesn't know tha you *swim* in a bathing suit," Littl Witch whispered. Bow-Wow rolle his eyes.

She climbed on her broomstick,
waved goodbye, and off she flew.

Little Witch landed at camp right next to the Camp Green Willow bus.

"Hi!" she said to a group of campers.

"A witch!" shrieked a girl named Martha.

"On a broomstick!" gasped a boy named Joey.

"Witches don't take buses," explained Little Witch.

Marcus got off the bus and ran to Little Witch. They were so happy to see each other! Little Witch and Marcus were both assigned to the Grape Group. The other children whispered and stared at Little Witch.

"Hello, campers!" said a lady with a whistle. "My name is Heidi. I am the Grape Group leader. And who are all of you?"

One by one the children said their names. When Little Witch said her name, some children giggled.

"What kind of silly name is that?" asked Elizabeth.

"It's *my* name," said Little Witch. She felt a little sad, but kept smiling anyway. "I guess she's never met a witch before," she whispered to Marcus.

The campers put their bathing suits and towels and lunch boxes in their cubbies in the Grape Group bunk.

“Okay, Grapes!” said Heidi. “Let’s start the day with a sing-along!”

“I love to sing!” said Little Witch. Heidi led the children to a beautiful meadow, and everyone sat in a circle. But they sang a song Little Witch had never heard before, called “The Bear Went over the Mountain,” so she couldn’t sing along.

Chloe giggled when Little Witch didn't know the words.
"*Everybody* knows that song," said Chloe.
Little Witch was so embarrassed! She tried not to cry.

After sing-along, Heidi said, “Calling all Grapes! Time for a swimming lesson!”

Everyone ran to the bunk to put on their bathing suits. Little Witch’s bathing suit didn’t look like anyone else’s.

“You look silly,” said Elizabeth.

“Do you know how to swim?” asked Chloe. “*I* do.”

“No,” said Little Witch. “But I can fly!”

Elizabeth laughed nastily. “Nobody can fly,” she said.

"Oh, no? Just watch," said Little Witch. She said a magic spell:

> "Campity shlampity,
> Pudding proof,
> Fly me to
> The Grape bunk roof!"

Whoosh! Little Witch zoomed up and landed on the roof. Everyone was shocked.

"Well," said Elizabeth finally, "that is still the ugliest bathing suit—I mean, *flying* suit—I've ever seen."

At lunchtime, Little Witch sat with Marcus. A big tear rolled down her cheek. She was too sad to eat. "Why are they so mean to me?" she said.

"Don't be sad!" said Marcus. "I bet they're jealous because you can fly."

After lunch, it was time for art. Little Witch loved to draw. She drew a picture of her family. Suddenly she missed them so much! Even Aunt Nasty was nicer than Elizabeth and Chloe. Little Witch couldn't wait to go home.

When Little Witch got home, all the witches were waiting for her.

"Did you make new friends?" asked Mother Witch.

"NO!" cried Little Witch. "Nobody likes me!"

"WONDERFUL!" said Mother Witch, clapping her hands. "I'm so proud of you. Were you mean to all the children?"

"No," said Little Witch. "THEY were mean to ME! They laughed at me!" She sat on the porch and cried and cried. Cousin Dippy began to cry, too.

"I think *you* should laugh at *them,*" said Aunt Grouchy.

"I think you should turn them all into worms!" shrieked Aunt Nasty.

When Little Witch went to bed, Mother Witch gave her an extra hug. Little Witch started to cry again.

"Stop crying," said Mother Witch. "You should be MAD, not SAD!"

"But I didn't know the song," cried Little Witch.

"SO WHAT? You'll learn it!" screamed Mother Witch.

"And nobody liked my bathing suit," said Little Witch with a sniffle.

"YOU like it," shrieked Mother Witch. "YOU'RE somebody!"

Little Witch began to smile. "That's true," she said.
"Be yourself," said Mother Witch. "And just think—tomorrow you'll have another chance to be ROTTEN!"

Little Witch flew back to camp the next morning. Today she remembered most of the words at sing-along, which made her happy.

"Okay, Grape Group!" said Heidi. "Let's go to the field and play some soccer!"

Uh-oh, thought Little Witch. She had never even heard of soccer. She asked Marcus what it was.

"It's a game with two teams. You kick a ball and try to get it past the person called the goalie, and the goalie tries to stop you. If you get the ball into the net, you score a goal. It's easy. Don't worry."

Chloe heard Marcus explaining soccer and howled with laughter.

"You don't know what *soccer* is? That is so DUMB!"

"Well, *now* she knows!" said Marcus. Little Witch smiled at him.

But soccer was not such an easy game. Little Witch did everything wrong. She tried to catch the ball with her hands. When she did, Heidi blew the whistle.

"You're not allowed to touch the ball with your hands unless you're the goalie," said Chloe in disgust. "You're making us lose!"

All the kids laughed at her. But Little Witch didn't pay attention. She'd had enough. "I think it's time for a little magic," she said. So she said a magic spell:

"Soccery dockery,
Goalie ick,
Make the goalie
Miss my kick!"

Little Witch gave the soccer ball the witchiest kick she could, and *zoom*—it flew right past the goalie and into the net.

"HURRAY!" shouted Chloe. "You scored a goal! Go, Little Witch!"

At lunch, Little Witch was very hungry. She sat with Marcus and Elizabeth and Chloe.

"You get *candy* for lunch?" said Elizabeth. "All I have is this boring cheese sandwich."

"I'll trade you," said Little Witch. "I'm SO sick of candy!"

Elizabeth smiled at Little Witch for the first time, and Little Witch smiled back.

At the end of the day, Little Witch couldn't *wait* to get home. But this time it was different. She was happy.

The witches were waiting on the porch.

"Were you mean to the children?" said Aunt Grouchy.

"Did you turn them into worms?" said Aunt Nasty.

"Are you going to cry again?" cried Cousin Dippy.

"No and no and no!" said Little Witch.

"So what DID you do?" yelled Mother Witch.

"I did what you told me to do. I was just me. And you know what? It was great!"

Mother Witch sighed. "I'm always right, aren't I?" she said. "I'm proud of you. You always prove how smart I am."

"I sure do," said Little Witch with a wink.